MEET THE COMMUNITY HELPERS!

A DAY WITH A DOCTOR

by Maria Tornito
illustrated by Dean Gray

GRASSHOPPER

Tools for Parents & Teachers

Grasshopper Books enhance imagination and introduce the earliest readers to fiction with fun storylines and illustrations. The easy-to-read text supports early reading experiences with repetitive sentence patterns and sight words.

Before Reading

- Discuss the cover illustration. What do they see?
- Look at the picture glossary together. Discuss the words.

Read the Book

- Read the book to the child, or have him or her read independently.
- "Walk" through the book and look at the illustrations. Who is the main character? What is happening in the story?

After Reading

- Prompt the child to think more. Ask: Nora sees Dr. Ali for a checkup. Why else might a child see Dr. Ali? Have you ever been to the doctor?

Grasshopper Books are published by Jump!
5357 Penn Avenue South
Minneapolis, MN 55419
www.jumplibrary.com

Library of Congress Cataloging-in-Publication Data

Names: Tornito, Maria, author. | Gray, Dean, illustrator.
Title: A day with a doctor / by Maria Tornito; illustrated by Dean Gray.
Description: Minneapolis, MN: Jump!, Inc., [2022]
Series: Meet the community helpers!
Includes reading tips and supplementary back matter.
Audience: Ages 5-8.
Identifiers: LCCN 2021000244 (print)
LCCN 2021000245 (ebook)
ISBN 9781636902104 (hardcover)
ISBN 9781636902111 (paperback)
ISBN 9781636902128 (ebook)
Subjects: LCSH: Readers (Primary)
Pediatricians–Juvenile fiction.
Classification: LCC PE1119.2 .T6728 2022 (print)
LCC PE1119.2 (ebook) | DDC 428.6/2–dc23
LC record available at https://lccn.loc.gov/2021000244
LC ebook record available at https://lccn.loc.gov/2021000245

Editor: Eliza Leahy
Direction and Layout: Anna Peterson
Illustrator: Dean Gray

Printed in the United States of America at Corporate Graphics in North Mankato, Minnesota.

Table of Contents

Nora's Day with Dr. Ali

Today, Nora has a checkup with her pediatrician.

Dr. Ali checks Nora's eyes.

"Do doctors do checkups all day?" Nora asks.

“I also help children when they are sick,” Dr. Ali says.

She uses a stethoscope to listen to Nora’s heart and lungs.

“Oh, yeah,” Nora says. “You gave me medicine when I had a cough.”

"That's right," Dr. Ali says. "Earlier, I helped a boy who fell off his bike. I stitched a cut on his arm. Now, sit still."

Dr. Ali checks Nora's reflexes.

Nora's leg jerks up.

"Weird!" says Nora.

"I gave another child a shot," Dr. Ali says.

"Yikes! I don't like shots," Nora says.

"Don't worry. You don't need any today. But shots can keep you from getting really sick," says Dr. Ali. "Now, say 'ah.'"

"AAAAAHHHHH!" Nora says loudly.

"Later, I'll visit two newborn babies at the hospital," says Dr. Ali. "I want to make sure they're doing well."

"I would love to visit babies!" Nora says.

“Then I have to do some paperwork,” Dr. Ali adds.

“That doesn’t sound fun,” says Nora. She sticks out her tongue.

"It's all part of my job to keep children healthy," Dr. Ali says. "And you, Nora, are healthy."

"Hurray!" Nora cheers.

"You did great! Would you like a sticker?" Dr. Ali asks.

"Yes, please," says Nora.

“Thanks, Dr. Ali,” says Nora. “Maybe one day I can be a pediatrician, too.”

Dr. Ali smiles. “I’m sure you can,” she says.

Quiz Time!

What does Dr. Ali do during the checkup to see if Nora is healthy?

A. gives her a shot B. fills out paperwork
C. checks her heart and lungs with a stethoscope
D. gives her medicine

Doctors' Supplies

These are some of the supplies Dr. Ali uses during Nora's checkup. Can you point to them in the book?

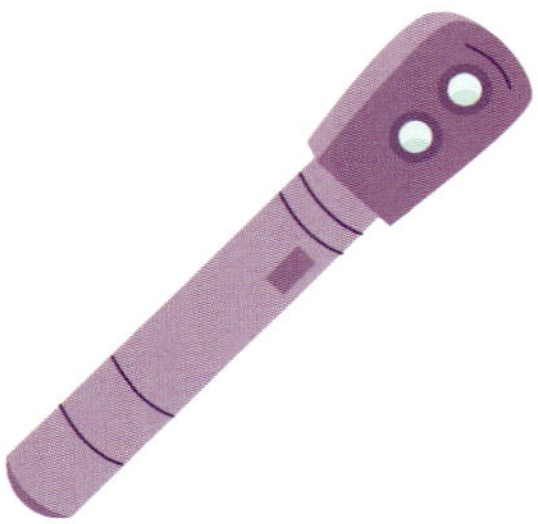

ophthalmoscope

otoscope

reflex hammer

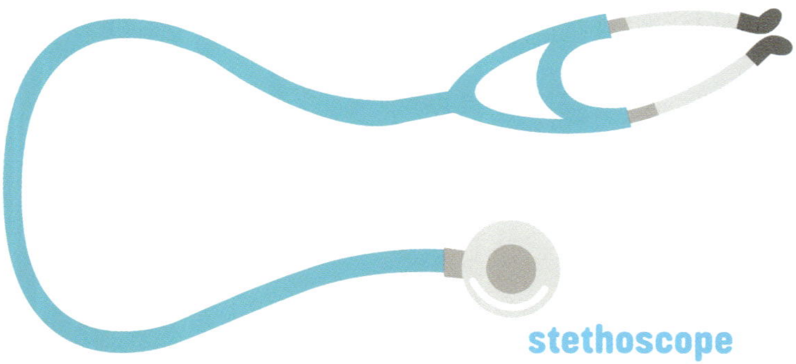

stethoscope

tongue depressor

Quiz Time! Answer Key: C. checks her heart and lungs with a stethoscope

Picture Glossary

checkup
A medical exam of a person to make sure he or she is healthy.

hospital
A place where hurt or sick people go to get medical treatment.

pediatrician
A doctor who specializes in caring for and treating babies and children.

reflexes
Automatic actions or movements that happen without a person's control.

Index

To Learn More

FACT SURFER

Finding more information is as easy as 1, 2, 3.

1. Go to www.factsurfer.com
2. Enter "**adaywithadoctor**" into the search box.
3. Choose your book to see a list of websites.